COLORING BOOK

MW00934696

THIS BOOK BELONGS TO

NATIVITY

COLORING BOOK

TEST COLORING PAGE

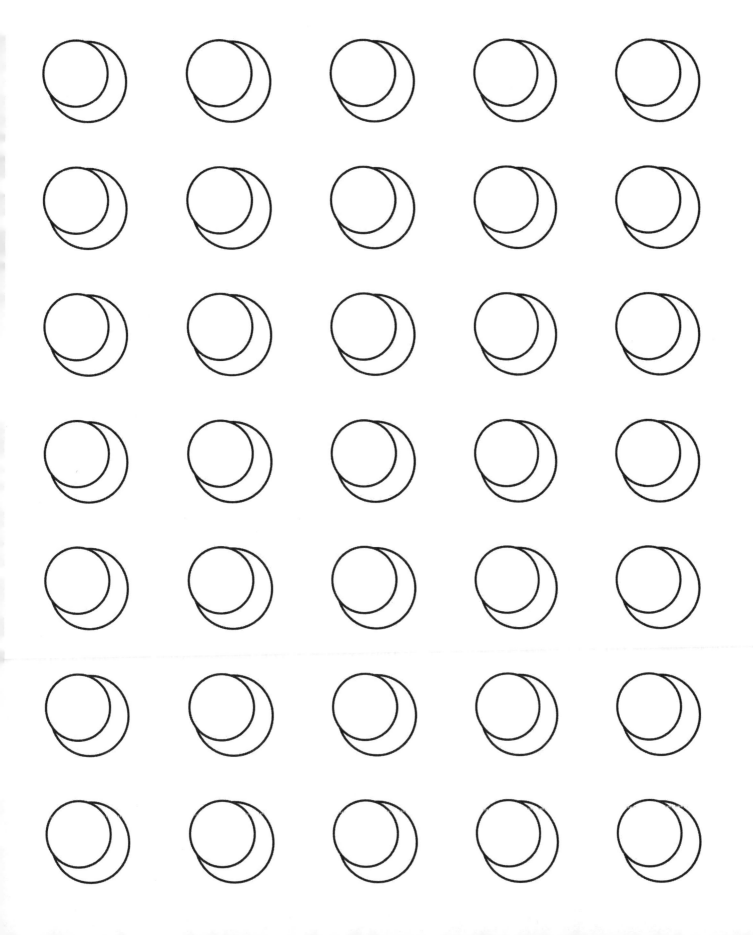

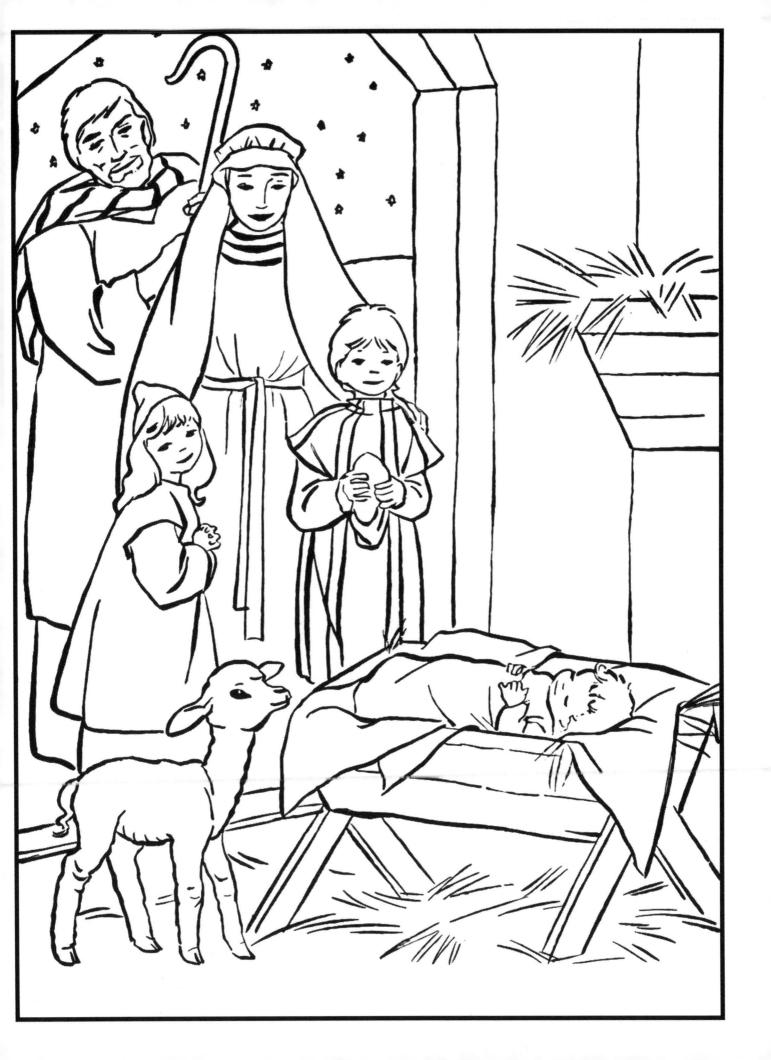

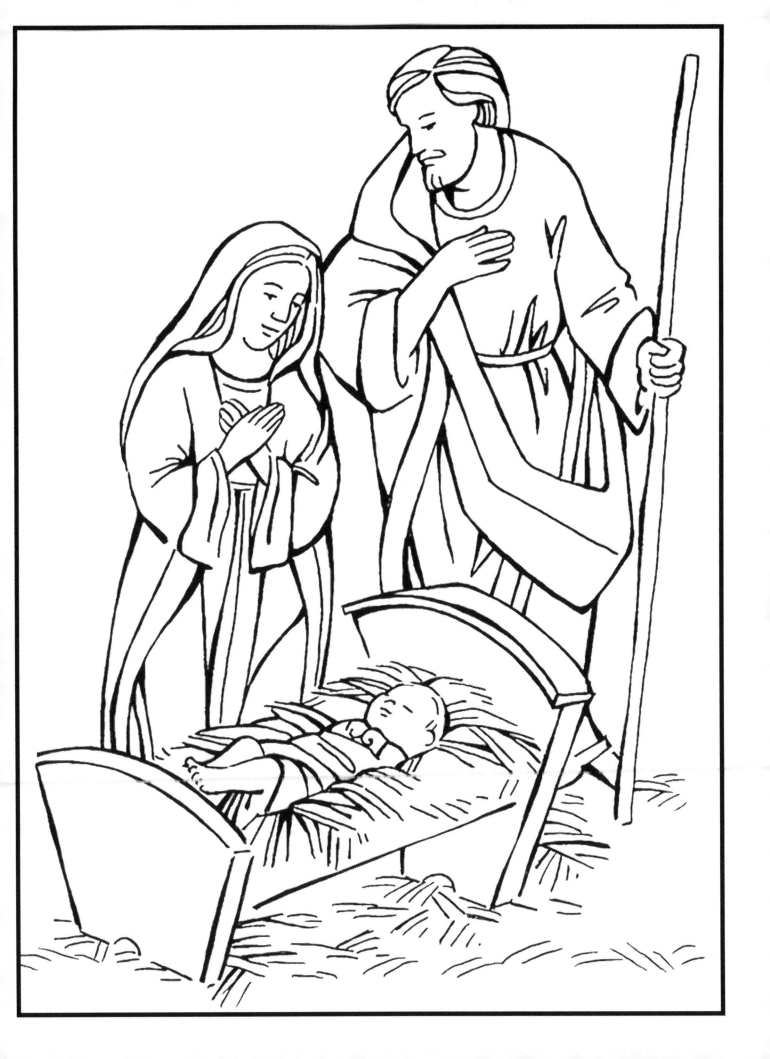

WRITE DOWN
WHAT YOU LIKE ABOUT THIS BOOK:

....

....

....

....

....

....

....

....

....

....

....

....

THANK YOU VERY MUCH FOR TRUSTING
AND CHOOSING OUR PRODUCT

WISH YOU ALL THE BEST
IN YOUR FUTURE

HOPE YOU WILL PUT YOUR TRUST
IN OUR NEXT PRODUCT

Made in the USA
Monee, IL
04 December 2024

72471476R00037